Anonymous

Annual Report of the Royal Edinburgh Asylum for the Insane: For the year 1858

Anatiposi

Anonymous

Annual Report of the Royal Edinburgh Asylum for the Insane: For the year 1858

Reprint of the original.

1st Edition 2023 | ISBN: 978-3-38230-512-3

Anatiposi Verlag is an imprint of Outlook Verlagsgesellschaft mbH.

Verlag (Publisher): Outlook Verlag GmbH, Zeilweg 44, 60439 Frankfurt, Deutschland
Vertretungsberechtigt (Authorized to represent): E. Roepke, Zeilweg 44, 60439 Frankfurt, Deutschland
Druck (Print): Books on Demand GmbH, In de Tarpen 42, 22848 Norderstedt, Deutschland

ANNUAL REPORT

OF THE

ROYAL EDINBURGH ASYLUM

FOR

THE INSANE.

FOR THE YEAR 1858.

EDINBURGH:
PRINTED AT THE ROYAL ASYLUM PRESS.

MDCCCLIX.

ROYAL EDINBURGH ASYLUM

FOR

THE INSANE.

Patroness—The Queen.

OFFICE-BEARERS FOR 1859.

GOVERNOR.
THE DUKE OF BUCCLEUCH AND QUEENSBERRY.

DEPUTY-GOVERNORS.

Sir George Clerk, Bart.
Sir John S. Forbes, Bart.
Chas. Cowan, Esq.
James Mackenzie, Esq.

EXTRAORDINARY MANAGERS.

Lord Provost of the City of Edinburgh
Lord President of the Court of Session.
Lord Justice-Clerk of the Court of Justiciary.
Lord Advocate of Scotland.
Solicitor-General of Scotland.
Dean of the Faculty of Advocates.
Deputy-Keeper of Her Majesty's Signet.
Members of Parliament for the City.
Member of Parliament for the County.

Sheriff of the County of Edinburgh.
Principal of the University of Edinburgh.
President of the Royal College of Physicians.
President of the Royal College of Surgeons.
Senior Minister of Edinburgh.
Master of the Merchant Company.
Preses of the Society of Solicitors.
Dean of Guild of the City.
Deacon Convener of the Trades.

ORDINARY MANAGERS.

The Lord Provost (*ex off.*)
Henry Craigie, Esq.
Dr David Wilson.
Dr Andrew.
Rev. Dr George Smith.
Bailie Blackadder.
L. A. Wallace, Esq.
Bailie Johnston.

James Taylor, Esq.
Alex. Fleming, Esq.
Adam Messer, Esq.
Dr Andrew Wood.
G. A. M'Laren, Esq.
Captain Mackay.
Major Petley.

MEDICAL BOARD.

President of the Royal College of Physicians.
President of the Royal College of Surgeons.

Dr William Pulteney Alison.
James Syme, Esq.
Dr David Maclagan.

Dr Gillespie, *Consulting Physician.*   Dr Skae, *Resident Physician.*

Dr John Sibbald, Dr J. Young, and Dr G. Williamson, *Medical Assistants.*

Matron.   Mr And. Leslie, *House Superintendent.*

Rev. R. Lorimer, *Chaplain.*

J. Scott, W.S., and D. S. Moncrieff, W.S., *Conjunct Treasurers and Secretaries.*

REPORT

OF

THE ORDINARY MANAGERS

OF THE

ROYAL EDINBURGH ASYLUM FOR THE INSANE.

*Presented to the Annual General Meeting of the Corporation,
held on 28th February, 1859.*

The Managers of the Asylum, in pursuance of the directions contained in their Act of Incorporation, have now to present an account of their proceedings during the past year, and of the condition of the Institution under their charge.

The average number of Patients in all departments of the Institution during the year 1858 was 645, being an increase of 52 over the average number of the preceding year.

This increase arises from the fact, that the new West Wing and detached building were not available for the accommodation of Patients until the latter part of the year 1857, while during the past year these as well as the other parts of the Asylum have been fully and constantly occupied.

The amount of the Ordinary Income during the
year was £19,890 4 7½
And of Ordinary Expenditure, . . . 18,825 5 9½

Thus leaving a Surplus Income of . . £1064 18 10

The Managers think it proper to state, that the above Ordinary Expenditure necessarily embraces the cost of provisions supplied and consumed during the last quarter of the year 1857, when prices were at an unusually high rate, and does not include the expense under this head during the last quarter of the past year, when a considerable reduction had taken place.

In accordance with the principles laid down in the scheme proposed by the Accountant for establishing the Sinking Fund, part of this surplus has been carried to the credit of the Sinking Fund Account.

The Managers have to report, that the Washing-house, Laundry, and other works which were in progress at the commencement of the year, have now been completed, and are found to be in every respect highly conducive to the comfort and well-being of the establishment.

In consequence of the expense attending these operations, the Managers have been unable during the past year to reduce their existing debt. In order to meet the provisions of the Act of Parliament in this respect, the sum of £571, 19s. 1d. has been borrowed, and simultaneously repaid, in manner recommended by the Accountant. By this means the borrowing powers of the Corporation under the Act have been exhausted, and the requirements of the Act at the same time fulfilled.

The Counties of Midlothian and Peebles having agreed to form themselves into a separate District under the provisions of the new Lunacy Act, and having, as it is believed, been advised by the Lord Advocate that they were necessitated to enter into arrangements with this Asylum for the reception and maintenance of the whole Pauper Lunatics belonging to the District, negociations with that view are now in progress between the Managers and the District, the result of which it would be premature to contemplate, but will be duly reported.

On the internal arrangements of the Asylum the Managers have nothing to report, except that during the past year matters have been conducted by the various officials of the Institution in such a manner as to command the approval of the Commissioners appointed under the Lunacy Act.

The rates of Board for Pauper Patients continue the same as last year, viz. £22 and £25 for privileged and non-privileged Patients respectively; and considering that the whole scale of Boards will require revision when the arrangements are concluded with the District Board, the Managers cannot recommend to the Corporation any change on the rates at present.

Along with the Accounts of the Treasurers, there are submitted the Accounts and Annual Report of the Committee appointed to administer the Charitable Fund of the Asylum, together with the Reports of the Physician-Superintendent and the Chaplain of the Institution.

In conclusion, the Managers desire to record a tribute of respect to the memory of their late venerable and lamented fellow-citizen, Alexander Cowan, Esquire, who for many years proved himself so warm a friend of the Institution, and by his repeated and well-timed donations, greatly assisted the Managers in carrying into effect some most important improvements tending to the well-being of the inmates of the Asylum.

ALEXANDER STEVENSON.

REPORT

OF THE

CHARITY COMMITTEE OF MANAGERS

OF THE

ROYAL EDINBURGH ASYLUM FOR THE INSANE,

FEBRUARY 28, 1859.

The Committee beg leave to submit to the Managers State of their Accounts for the last year, in reference to the Fund under their charge.

The whole cases receiving aid at the date of last Report still continue to enjoy the benefit of the fund. The only additional case, during the past year, was that of a Patient who, after due consideration, was put upon the roll during the period of one quarter, after which she was removed upon her recovery.

The amount of the Fund is at present £5338 13s. 6d.

HENRY CRAIGIE, *Convener.*

ABSTRACT

OF THE

TREASURERS' ACCOUNT

FOR THE YEAR 1858.

I. CHARGE.

1. Adjusted Balance due by Treasurer at 31st December,
   1857, ... L.532 15 4
2. Arrears of Board given up in last Account, . . 203 15 7
3. Patients' Boards, ... , . 18,977 9 10
4. Furnishings made to Patients, &c. . . . 371 13 8½
5. Rents of Land and Houses, ... 14 15 0
6. Produce sold, ... 483 2 4
7. Miscellaneous, ... 48 4 9
8. Balance due to Treasurers at 31st December, 1858, . 1878 17 4

Amount of Charge, . L.22,510 13 10½

II. DISCHARGE.

I. Ordinary Expenditure.
  1. Annual Disbursements for the Institution—
    (1.) Provisions, . L.8761 12 3
    (2.) Repairs and Fur-
        nishings, includ-
        ing Grounds, 4729 4 0
    (3.) Public and Paro-
        chial Burdens, 163 5 8
    (4.) Interests, . 1224 11 6½
    (5.) Feu-duty, . 393 5 11
    (6.) Insurance against
        Fire, . . 24 17 1
    (7.) Miscellaneous Pay-
        ments, . . 155 2 6
        Carry forward, ———— L.15,451 18 11½ L.22,510 13 10½

Amount of Charge brought forward,   L.22,510 13 10½

II. DISCHARGE—*Continued.*

Brought forward,   L.15,451 18 11½

2. Salaries, &c.:—

1. Resident Physician,	. L.460	0	0	
2. Assistant ditto, .	. 52	19	8	
3. Second Assistant ditto,	53	19	0	
4. Third Assistant ditto,	13	12	2	
5. Consulting ditto,	. 25	4	0	
6. Matron, . .	. 105	0	0	
7. Chaplain, . .	. 80	0	0	
8. House Superintendent,	80	0	0	
9. Gardeners,	. . 52	10	0	
10. Gatekeeper,	. . 31	10	0	
11. Honorarium to Visiting Committee, . .	110	0	0	
12. Conjunct Treasurers and Secretaries, .	. 380	0	0	
13. Attendants, &c. .	. 1954	7	1	

     3399 1 11

3. Expense of New Buildings,   .   .   3376 13 9

4. Arrears of Boards outstanding,   .   282 19 3

Amount of Discharge,   ————— L.22,510 13 10½

ABSTRACT

OF THE

ORDINARY INCOME AND EXPENDITURE.

I. INCOME.

1. Boards, ...	L.18,977 9 10
2. Furnishings to Patients, &c.	371 13 8½
3. Rents, ...	14 15 0
4. Produce, ...	483 2 4
5. Miscellaneous, ...	48 4 9
Amount of Income, . .	L.19,895 5 7½
Carry forward,	L.19,895 5 7½

Amount of Income brought forward,   L.19,895 5 7½

II. EXPENDITURE.

1. Ordinary—
   1. Disbursements and Annual Payments,
      as before,   .   .   . L.15,451 18 11½
   2. Salaries, ...   3399 1 11
                                18,851 0 10½

Surplus of Ordinary Income over Ordinary Expenditure, L 1044 4 9

STATE OF FUNDS AT 31st DECEMBER, 1858.

I. DEBTS.

1. Amount of Debts on Bonds and Dispositions in Security, ... L.28.028 0 11
2. Accounts for the Quarter ended, .   .   3299 3 10½
3. Outstanding Accounts, and proportion of current Feu-Duty, Interest, Taxes, &c., say .   .   350 0 0
4. Balance due to Treasurers, .   .   . 1878 17 4
                         L.33,556 2 1½

II. ASSETS.

1. Arrears of Boards, as before, . . L.282 19 3
2. Provisions and Stock on hand, . . 1000 1 2½
                         1283 0 5½

Deficiency, . . L.32,273 1 8

ABSTRACT

OF THE

TREASURERS' INTROMISSIONS

WITH THE

FUNDS OF THE CHARITY COMMITTEE,

FOR THE YEAR 1858.

I. CHARGE.

1. Balance in Treasurer's hands at 31st December, 1857, .	L.940	5 8
2. Donation from the late Alexander Cowan, Esq., . .	1000	0 0
3. Donation received from the Earl of Stair, . .	2	0 0
4. Interests, ...	190	12 10

Amount of Charge,   .   .   L.2132 18   6

II. DISCHARGE.

Sum paid to account of Patients' Boards, ...   L.94   5   0

Balance in Treasurers' hands at 31st December, 1858,   L.2038 13   6

STATE OF FUNDS AT 31st DECEMBER, 1858.

1. Amount held in Loan by the Managers of the Asylum,   L.3300   0   0
2. Balance in Treasurers' hands, per preceding Account,   2038 13   6

L.5338 13   6

ABSTRACT OF THE ACCOUNTS

OF THE

ROYAL EDINBURGH ASYLUM

FOR THE

EARS 1856 AND 1857, SEPARATING THE CAPITAL FROM THE REVENUE, AND SHEWING THE OPERATION OF THE SINKING FUND.

I. REVENUE ACCOUNT.

CHARGE.	1856.			1857.			TOTAL.		
	L.	S.	D.	L.	S.	D.	L.	S.	D.
lance of Revenue on hand at 31st December, 1855, ...	...			...			425	15	3
rears of Board at 31st Dec., 1855, .	...			...			192	13	2
tients' Boards, ...	16,229	5	10	17,710	14	4			
tra Accounts, ...	341	18	5	199	2	1			
nts, ...	56	19	6	29	15	10			
oduce sold, ...	384	17	6	36J	8	7½			
iscellaneous Receipts, . . .	27	18	0						
terest received on Bank Account, &c.,	286	9	9	119	14	4			
	17,327	9	0	18,428	15	2½			
				17.327	9	0			
							35,756	4	2½
							36,374	12	7½

DISCHARGE.									
isbursements and Annual Payments for Provisions, Furnishin's. &c., deducting Interests paid, 1856, L.885 17s. 8d.; 1857. L.1093 18s. 1d., . .	12,021	0	1½	12,957	1	9			
alaries of Officers and Attendants' Wages, ...	3123	11	6½	3234	5	2			
nking Fund Instalments, 2½ years to Martinmas 1857 inclusive, and Interest due thereon, ...	...			3792	15	10			
	15,144	11	8	19,984	2	9			
				15,144	11	8			
				35,128	14	5			
rrears of Board at 31st December, 1857, . .				203	15	7			
							35,332	10	0
Balance in favour of Revenue at 31st December, 1857,							£1042	2	7½

II. CAPITAL ACCOUNT.

CHARGE.	1856.			1857.			Total	
	L.	S.	D.	L.	S.	D.	L.	S.
Balance of Capital on hand at 31st December, 1855,		...			...		*9028	1
Loan received,	900	0	0					
Cash lent repaid,	2100	0	0					
Subscriptions for new Washing-house and Laundry,		...		60	15	7		
Loan received per Sinking Fund Account,		...		1400	0	0		
	3000	0	0	1460	15	7		
				3000	0	0		
							4460	15
							13,488	16
DISCHARGE.								
Payments for New Buildings and Furniture,	8460	15	0	2971	15	5		
Price of Property at Tipperlinn purchased,		...		480	0	0		
Cash lent,	100	0	0					
	10,560	15	0	3451	15	5		
				10,560	15	0		
							14,012	10

Balance against Capital at 31st December, 1857, . . £523 13

III. SINKING FUND ACCOUNT.

CHARGE.

One Year's instalment due at Martinmas 1856, effeiring to L.28 028 of debt, taking the rate of interest at 4½ per cent., ... L.1720

Add for the half year to Martinmas 1855, being the difference between L.860, the amount of the Sinking Fund, and L.546, the interest paid for the corresponding term, ... 314

Carry forward, . . L.2034

---

* The above balance is composed thus:—
Amount borrowed, as at 31st December, 1854, . . L.12,400 0 0
Borrowed in 1855 (L.19,228, 0s. 11d.—L.4500), . . 14,728 0 11

L.27,128 0 11

Whereof expended on new buildings in 1855, L.5226 12 0
Expended prior to 1855, . . 12,873 7 8½

18,099 19 8

Balance on hand, as above, . . L.9028 1 2

Amount of Charge brought forward, . L.2034 0 0
erest to Martinmas 1857, at 4½ per cent., on L.862, being balance of the
above sum, after payment of L.1172, the interest, as stated below, . 38 15 10

L.2072 15 10
talment due at Martinmas 1857, ... 1720 0 0

L.3792 15 10

DISCHARGE.

erest paid on Loans—
Year to Martinmas 1856, per account 1856, . . L.1172 7 5
Year to Martinmas 1857, per account 1857, . . 1206 2 1

L.2378 9 6
an paid off, being new loan held to have been contracted
'or the Asylum, and thus repaid from Sinking Fund, . 1400 0 0
————— 3778 9 6

Balance in favour of Sinking Fund at 31st Dec., 1857, . . L.14 6 4

As the Accounts of the Asylum embrace the Interests from Martinmas to Martinmas
nually, it will keep matters more distinct to make the instalments of the Sinking Fund
vable at Martinmas yearly instead of Whitsunday, and this plan has accordingly been
opted in the preceding State; the first half year's instalment due at Martinmas 1855,
rather the surplus thereof, after deducting the corresponding interest paid, being
ted separately.
At Martinmas 1858 the Sinking Fund must be increased so as to correspond with the
reased amount of Cash borrowed, namely, L.29,428. (See State of Debt.)

V. SUMMARY OF BALANCES ARISING ON THE FOREGOING ACCOUNTS, AT 31ST DECEMBER, 1857.

Due to Sinking Fund Account, . . . L.14 6 4
Due to Revenue Account, ... 1042 2 7½

L.1056 8 11½
Due by Capital Account, ... 523 13 7½

Nett balance due by Treasurer, . . L.532 15 4

V. STATE OF DEBT AT 31ST DECEMBER, 1857.

nount borrowed, as at 31st December, 1855, ... L.27,128 0 11
rrowed on 1st January, 1856, ... 900 0 0

L.28,028 0 11
ditional loan contracted at 11th November, 1857, as before stated, . 1400 0 0

Total amount borrowed under Act of Parliament, L.29,428 0 11
duct loan repaid on 11th November, 1857, as before stated, . 1400 0 0

Balance due at 31st December, 1857, . . L.28,028 0 11

Edinburgh, 26th February, 1859.—Certified by   THOS. MARTIN, C.A.

PHYSICIAN'S ANNUAL REPORT

OF THE

ROYAL EDINBURGH ASYLUM FOR THE INSANE,

FOR THE YEAR 1858.

*Read at the Annual Meeting of Contributors, held on the
28th day of February,* 1859.

In submitting to you my Report of the history of the Asylum
during the past year, I think it my first duty to record, with devout
gratitude, that the general health of the community was excellent,
that they were visited by no epidemic, and that no suicide or other
casualty occurred to cast a gloom over the prevailing tranquillity
of the place.

The general results of the past year are exhibited in the following
Table :—

TABLE I.—*General Results of the Year.*

	Males.	Females.	TOTAL.
Number of inmates at the close of 1857,	348	291	639
Admitted during the year 1858, . . .	118	117	235
Total number under treatment, . .	466	408	874
Discharged, M. F. T. 76 82 = 158.			
M. F. T. Of whom were Cured, . 47 44 = 91			
... ... Uncured, 29 38 = 67			
Deaths, . 48 26 = 74			
	124	108	232
Total number at the close of 1858, .	342	300	642

Average number daily resident during the year 1858.

Males.	Females.	Total.
$343\frac{66}{365}$	$300\frac{249}{365}$	$643\frac{315}{365}$

C

From this tabular statement the following facts may be deduced :—

At the close of the year 1857, the number of patients remaining in the Asylum was 639, and there have been admitted during the past year 235, so that the total number who have been under treatment amounts to 874. Of this number 232 have been removed, leaving 642 inmates at the close of the year 1858. The average daily number resident during the year was 646.

Notwithstanding the large number of admissions, I was reluctantly compelled to refuse admission to upwards of 173, of whom 66 were males, and 107 females. The very large number of females refused in proportion to males arises from the circumstance of the north-west wing of the Western Department which is allotted for females being yet unbuilt. This is the only portion of the Western house which remains to be erected, in order to complete the building, and its erection would afford not only accommodation for an additional number of females, which appears to be much required, but would also afford increased facilities for a more satisfactory classification of the various cases, than is at present available in the female department.

Of the 188 patients discharged, 91 were cured, and 67 uncured. The recoveries, it will thus be seen, were in the ratio of 38·72 per cent. to the numbers admitted, or 15·63 per cent. to the average number of inmates. The proportion of recoveries is greater than that of the preceding year, a fact easily explained by the circumstance, that during the previous year, owing to the opening of additional accommodation, fewer patients were refused, and a larger number of incurable cases were consequently received.

During the transition state of matters now existing, under the operation of the new Lunacy Act for Scotland, a large number of old and hopeless cases of insanity, which have been confined for years in Private Asylums, workhouses, or boarded with their friends, or otherwise improperly provided for, must continue to be poured into the Public Asylums as provision is made for their reception, and thus the apparent proportion of recoveries compared with the admissions, must continue for some years to appear much smaller than it did under the old laws, when no such cause operated. Nevertheless the proportion of cures is highly satisfactory when compared with that of other institutions; and if calculated upon, the recent and curable cases will be seen to be very large indeed, shewing that the resources and treatment of the Asylum answer the most sanguine expectations which could be entertained in regard to the benefits it confers on the insane. Thus, for example, if the cases of Mania are separated from the others, as can be done by referring to a subsequent Table (Table IV.), and the recoveries (Table VII.) from this form of insanity, of which the cases are necessarily recent, be compared with the number admitted, it will be found that the recoveries amount to upwards of 67 per cent.

The number of patients admitted into the Asylum since it was opened now amounts to 4389. Of these 1807 have recovered, giving a ratio of 41·1 per cent. of recoveries on the total number admitted, or 48·2 per cent., deducting those who still remain under treatment.

The mortality was rather greater than that of the preceding year, but much less than that of many former years. It amounted to 11·4 per cent. of the mean number resident, or 8·4 per cent. on the total number under treatment.

Sixty-seven patients were removed uncured. The duration of their residence in the Asylum is given in the following Table :—

TABLE II.—*Period of Residence of those Uncured at their Removal.*

PERIOD OF RESIDENCE.	Males.	Females.	TOTAL.
One day, . . .	0	1	1
One week, . . .	1	0	1
Under 1 month, . .	0	1	1
,, 2 ,, . .	1	1	2
,, 3 ,, . .	2	0	2
,, 4 ,, . .	4	0	4
,, 5 ,, . .	3	2	5
,, 6 ,, . .	2	4	6
,, 7 ,, . .	0	2	2
,, 8 ,, . .	1	3	4
,, 9 ,, . .	3	0	3
,, 10 ,, . .	1	0	1
,, 12 ,, . .	0	2	2
,, 2 years, . .	7	10	17
,, 3 ,, . .	2	6	8
,, 4 ,, . .	1	2 .	3
,, 6 ,, . .	0	1	1
,, 9 ,, . .	0	2	2
,, 15 ,, . .	0	2	2
Total, . .	28	39	67

The first case in this Table, that of a female who was removed within twenty-four hours after her admission, was one admitted on a certificate of *emergency*, under a wise provision of the new statute, but whose friends, notwithstanding the emergency of the case, were unable to procure a warrant from the Sheriff. The warrant was refused because the facts upon which the medical men founded their opinion of the lady's insanity, and which now require to be specified in the certificates, were not such as, in the opinion of the Sheriff, amounted to proofs of insanity.

The second case in the foregoing Table, that of a man removed within a week after his admission, was one in which an act of homicide had been committed by the individual, and he was removed to jail to await his trial for murder. This case affords an illustration, along with others which occur every year, of the want of a proper Criminal Lunatic Asylum for Scotland. The admission of such a case even for a week into the wards of a general Asylum, and although the man was associated with paupers, exercises a most baneful influence upon the feelings of the other patients. It not only leads them to ascribe their deprivation of liberty to unjust charges against them, and to regard themselves as prisoners, but tends to engender in their minds a feeling of degradation and resentment at the idea of being associated with murderers.

This was not the only instance which occurred during the year bearing upon the same point. A young man was tried for murder, and acquitted on the ground that he was insane at the time he committed the act, although admitted to be sane at the time of his trial. The friends of this individual soon afterwards applied for his admission into the Asylum, and were refused for the reasons which have always guided us in reference to such cases, that it was not fair to admit into the house to associate with the other patients persons who had been brought to public trial for crimes such as murder. The result is, if other public institutions have acted on the same principle—and they appear generally to have done so heretofore, for the reasons mentioned—that this young man, although his friends are possessed of ample means to provide for his accommodation as a gentleman, surrounded with the amenities of life, and although he is now quite sane, may be compelled to reside in the

General Prison at Perth during her Majesty's pleasure, surrounded with all the horrors of a prison, and the additional horrors, as the prison admits of no classification, of living in immediate contact, by day and by night, with criminal lunatics in every stage of mental degradation. Such cases as these call loudly for the establishment of a Criminal Lunatic Asylum for Scotland, where the inmates, although all chargeable with offences against the laws, would at least enjoy the amenities afforded to other insane persons, and where those who have recovered their sanity, although still held in confinement in consequence of the legal difficulties and delays consequent upon their violence, would enjoy comforts suitable to their rank in life, and a reasonable amount of liberty and happiness, instead of being herded in a common prison ward with everything that can irritate the feelings and shock the senses.

Another of the uncured removals was an Irish pauper transferred like an ordinary pauper, by the order of a Justice of the Peace, to his native country. I mention this case as illustrative of a defect of our statutes regarding the insane, wherein no provision has yet been made for the transference of the insane poor of England or Ireland to Asylums in their respective countries, the consequence of which is, that when simply transferred as paupers, they are not unfrequently left at large, whether safe or unsafe, and have sometimes even begged their way back to Edinburgh, attracted by some natural ties.

Some of the removals were occasioned by the necessity for providing increased accommodation for the pauper lunatics of the district, a necessity which must probably lead ere long, under the new statute, to the removal of a very considerable number of the present inmates belonging to other districts.

When arrangements have been made for the reception of all the pauper insane of the Edinburgh District into this Asylum, the statistics will probably be materially modified in future years;—the number of incurables permanently resident will be increased, and the annual number of recent and curable cases will be diminished.

Table III. shews the ages of those admitted, of those who recovered, and of those who died.

TABLE III.—*Ages of those Admitted, Discharged Recovered, and Dead.*

AGE.	ADMITTED.			DISCHARGED RE-COVERED.			DEAD.		
	Males.	Females.	Total.	Males.	Females.	Total.	Males.	Females.	Total.
From 10 to 20, .	7	3	10	2	1	3	2	0	2
„ 20 „ 30, .	29	37	66	15	16	31	4	6	10
„ 30 „ 40, .	31	26	57	14	8	22	18	6	24
„ 40 „ 50, .	24	32	56	4	10	14	3	10	13
„ 50 „ 60, .	16	11	27	9	6	15	12	2	14
„ 60 „ 70, .	8	6	14	3	3	6	6	2	8
„ 70 „ 80, .	2	2	4	0	0	0	3	0	3
„ 80 „ 90, .	1	0	1	0	0	0	0	0	0
Total, . .	118	117	235	47	44	91	48	26	74

In Table IV. the cases admitted are classified according to the form of insanity under which they laboured at the time of admission.

TABLE IV.—*Form of Disease in those Admitted.*

FORM OF DISEASE.	Males.	Females.	TOTAL.
Mania, ...	21	17	38
„ Acute, ...	14	21	35
„ Chronic, . . .	1	0	1
„ Periodic, . . .	1	2	3
„ Hysterical, . . .	0	1	1
„ Puerperal, . . .	0	2	2
„ Epileptic, . . .	1	2	3
Melancholia, ...	15	24	39
„ Puerperal, . .	0	3	3
Dementia, ...	14	15	29
„ Senile, . . .	1	1	2
„ Epileptic, . .	1	1	2
Monomania of Fear, . .	2	1	3
„ Pride, . .	2	2	4
„ Suspicion, .	3	4	7
„ Unseen Agency,	5	8	13
„ Superstition, .	2	2	4
Moral Insanity, . . .	0	3	3
Do. in the form of Dipsomania,	4	4	8
Delirium Tremens, . . .	2	1	3
Hypochondriasis, . . .	1	0	1
Congenital Imbecility, . .	4	1	5
Idiocy, ...	1	0	1
General Paralysis, . . .	23	2	25
	118	117	235

A few of the singular fancies of our new inmates are perhaps interesting enough to be recorded. We have had an addition to our numerous royal family in a King of Scotland, and a Queen. One of our new friends believes that he is entirely made of silver; he walks very carefully lest he should break himself, and threatens to strike any one who ventures to touch him, he is so afraid of being broken or tarnished. A third is a spirit living in the next world, surrounded by spirits who see through him, and old friends and objects, such as Arthur's Seat, he recognises very like persons or things he had once known in the world below. A fourth believes, that in consequence of the dereliction of some duty to his wife, he has brought a large amount of evil upon the world at large, and that, in particular, he was the cause of large cities, of this Asylum, and of hats and striped shirts. Another resembles in every particular the wizards who were so cruelly treated in former years. He consulted a professed wizard about the sickness of his cows, and ever afterwards felt himself possessed by a demon who resides in his chest.

One woman believes herself to be the impotent man mentioned in the Acts of the Apostles, and thinks all the men she sees are women; while two other females, with an equally strange perversion of the judgment, believe all the women they see to be men.

In strong contrast with these and similar cases, were two who, with all the violence, and loquacity, and destructiveness, and filth of maniacs, exhibited no delusions whatever, but were clear and coherent, and full of wit, in all their noisy and incessant clamour.

The number of cases of General Paralysis continues to be unusually large, so much so, as to induce the belief that this hopeless and distressing disease is increasing in frequency. Two of the 25 cases admitted were females.

Four of the cases of this disease, now under treatment, presented a remarkable remission of some months' duration, during which the patients were apparently sane, being perfectly correct in their demeanour, and rational in their conversation. This temporary recovery, as it might be called, I have before witnessed in several instances, and I notice it here for three reasons; 1st, because I do not think it has been described before by others; 2dly, because it explains the very few exceptional cases in which this fatal disease has been reported by one or two writers as having been cured; and, 3dly, because it has important legal bearings upon the validity of deeds executed during such a remission, or the responsibility for crimes committed at such a time. This latter relation of the subject is a very difficult one, and was the source of much conflicting medical evidence in one or two important trials respecting property which took place during the past year. In these cases the gentlemen concerned undoubtedly laboured under General Paralysis, as the subsequent progress of the cases proved; but their mental condition at the time they were examined by several medical men was such, as to baffle them in their efforts to discover any mental impairment, even although more than one of these medical men were experts. This conflicting testimony is explained by such cases as those which I have referred to. In one of them the apparent recovery was so complete, that the patient was removed, and for a short time resumed and conducted his business, but ere long he returned to the Asylum. In another, the gentleman was removed by his friends, and after residing for some months with his wife, she was so convinced of his complete recovery, that she consulted me about the propriety of his going abroad and resuming his professional duties. This I dissuaded her from assenting to, and in a few weeks it was found necessary again to place him in confinement. I have been consulted in more than one case of the same kind as this in somewhat similar circumstances.

In all these cases the recovery I think is apparent and partial only; so much, that the person is considered sane by an ordinary observer, judging of his sanity from an ordinary conversation; but by those familiar with the phases of this curious disease, the curtain is readily drawn aside, and the mental deterioration unmasked. The persistence of the disease is seen not only in the impaired speech, and unsteady gait, and inexpressive face, but in the facile disposition, impaired energies, and the inability, when tested, to execute any task, even of a simple and familiar kind, requiring the continued exercise of thought and attention. A letter written on any subject requiring a little reflection or judgment, will probably exhibit the utter prostration of the reasoning faculties. In the case already referred to, when the patient's wife wished him to return to his duties abroad, where he had distinguished himself, it was found that, when he was permitted to try his skill on the same duties at home as a matter of amusement, he could not complete the simplest work assigned to him.

Two of the cases of General Paralysis admitted, instead of presenting the form of insanity so common to this disease, that of exaltation and the belief in imaginary wealth and grandeur, were associated with deep melancholy and depression, and one of them with a gradually increasing imbecility, dating from the commencement of the disease.

Three of the patients admitted came to the Asylum spontaneously, entreating to be received, one seeking refuge from imaginary foes and terrors, and the others security from acts of self-destruction to which they felt themselves impelled. Two of the three had formerly been inmates of the Asylum.

One of the cases admitted had already committed the act destined to end her cares, having swallowed a large quantity of laudanum. She was found asleep and insensible in a common stair by a kind and intelligent policeman, by whom she was promptly conveyed to the Infirmary, and there relieved of the poison.

The suicidal propensity was more frequently manifested, in proportion to the number of cases, than during any former year. Fortunately, however, no accident occurred from this deplorable impulse during the year.

The following Table illustrates the prevalence of this impulse in those admitted, the forms of insanity in which it shewed itself, and the various means used in the suicidal attempts which were actually made :—

TABLE V.—*Illustrations of Suicidal Tendency in those Admitted.*

	Males.	Females.	TOTAL.
Had attempted Suicide, . . .	14	13	27
Had meditated Suicide, . . .	14	18	32
Total, . . .	28	31	59
Form of Insanity during which Suicide was attempted—			
Acute Mania, ...	1	1	2
Mania, ...	2	0	2
Melancholia, ...	7	6	13
Dementia, ...	1	3	4
Monomania of Suspicion, . .	1	0	1
„ Unseen Agency, .	1	1	2
Moral Insanity, ...	0	2	2
General Paralysis, . . .	1	0	1
Total, . . .	14	13	27
Form of Insanity during which Suicide was meditated—			
Mania, ...	1	2	3
„ Acute, ...	1	1	2
„ Epileptic, . . .	0	1	1
Melancholia, ...	3	9	12
Dementia, ...	2	1	3
Monomania of Fear, . . .	2	1	3
„ Suspicion, . .	1	0	1
„ Unseen Agency, .	0	2	2
Dipsomania, ...	3	0	3
General Paralysis, . . .	1	1	2
Total, . . .	14	18	32
Means used in attempts made—			
Strangulation, ...	3	8	11
Suspension, ...	2	1	3
Precipitation, ...	4	1	5
Cut Throat, ...	2	3	5
Drowning, ...	2	1	3
Poisoning, ...	1	2	3
Starvation, ...	3	1	4
Stabbing, ...	1	0	1
Burning, ...	0	1	1
Total, . . .	18	18	36

In the next Table the causes of the disease, in each case, are enumerated, so far as they could be ascertained.

TABLE VI.—*Causes of Disease in those Admitted.*

CAUSE OF DISEASE.	Males.	Females.	TOTAL.
Hereditary, ...	14	21	35
Congenital, ...	5	1	6
Previous Attack, . . .	26	34	60
Disappointment, . . ,	2	0	2
Grief, ...	1	0	1
Terror, ...	1	4	5
Anxiety, ...	3	4	7
Remorse, ...	0	1	1
Success, , . . .	1	0	1
Excitement, ...	0	1	1
Disappointment in Love,	2	4	6
Domestic Affliction, . .	2	5	7
Losses in Business, . .	4	0	4
Over-study, ...	1	2	3
Prostitution, . . ,	0	1	1
Intemperance, . . .	16	10	26
Hot Climate, , . .	2	0	2
Injury to Head, . . .	4	1	5
Old Age, ...	1	1	2
Bad Health, ...	2	1	3.
Amenorrhœa, . . .	0	1	1
Change of Life, . . .	0	5	5
Over-Lactation, . . .	0	1	1
Secret Vice, . . .	3	1	4
Child-bearing, . . .	0	4	4
Cancer, ...	1	0	1
Epilepsy, . . . ,	1	3	4
Unknown, ...	41	30	71
Total, . .	133	136	269

From this statistical record, it appears that hereditary predisposition was acknowledged in 35 cases. This is far from giving the actual amount of the cases in which a hereditary taint existed, as no fact is more carefully concealed or ignored by friends in general than this.

The large number of 60 had suffered from previous attacks, and laboured therefore under a strong predisposition to the disease, so frequent are relapses.

Intemperance was ascribed as a cause in 26 cases, being in the ratio of 11 per cent. to the admissions, or 1 in 9. This is a larger ratio than that of the previous year, but materially less than in most of the years preceding it.

Some of the special or accidental causes of insanity have a popular interest, and are therefore deserving of notice. One man, who had been ill for about three years, and whose disease has taken the form of organic disease of the brain, owed it to a fall into that unprotected gap on the sea-side road at Newhaven, so well known under the name of "the man-trap." Another became insane under the excitement occasioned by the pulpit eloquence of a well-known and very estimable lay preacher. Four females became insane from sudden fears; one from seeing a brother fall over a window, another from seeing the body of a man mangled in a railway accident, a third from the terror occasioned by the great fire on the Mound, and a fourth from the terror and excitement of seeing her own husband attempting to cut his throat, from whose hand she, however, snatched the razor before he had committed the act. One interesting young female became insane from joy at getting a situation as a governess, for which she had been for some time striving, and in which attempt she had met with several disappointments. I need hardly add, it was her first success. Another female, who had been born and spent all her life in the lonely island of Uist, the *ultima thule* of Scotland, came to Edinburgh to visit her friends, and unfortunately arrived at the time of a great masonic procession. She was dragged through the streets of Edinburgh by her kind friends for several hours, to witness this grand pageant, and the excitement to the poor young woman, who had never before seen anything but Shetland sheep and ponies, proved so great, that she was brought to the Asylum the same evening in a state of raving mania.

The next Table exhibits the form of insanity in those who were discharged cured, and also of those who were uncured at the time of their removal.

TABLE VII.—*Diseases of those Cured and Uncured at their Removal.*

FORM OF DISEASE.	CURED.			UNCURED.		
	Males.	Fem.	TOTAL.	Males.	Fem.	TOTAL.
Mania, ...	14	7	21	5	4	9
„ Acute, . . .	10	18	28	1	1	2
„ Periodic, . . .	0	1	1	0	2	2
„ Puerperal, . .	0	1	1	0	0	0
„ Epileptic, . .	1	0	1	0	1	1
Melancholia, . . .	11	9	20	3	11	14
Dementia, ...	2	0	2	4	10	14
„ Epileptic, . .	0	0	0	0	1	1
Monomania of Fear, . .	0	1	1	0	0	0
„ Pride, . .	0	0	0	1	2	3
„ Suspicion, .	3	2	5	3	1	4
„ Unseen Agency,	0	1	1	1	3	4
Moral Insanity, . . .	1	2	3	0	0	0
Dipsomania, . . .	3	1	4	2	2	4
Delirium Tremens, . .	2	1	3	0	0	0
Imbecility, ...	0	0	0	4	0	4
General Paralysis, . .	0	0	0	3	1	4
Hypochondriasis, . .	0	0	0	1	0	1
	47	44	91	28	39	67

The results exhibited in this Table differ in no material point from those of former years. The more acute and violent forms of insanity are those most readily cured, and the more chronic, and quiet, and imbecile, the least curable. The recoveries from Moral Insanity, although amounting to cent. per cent. of the admissions, are the least satisfactory of any recoveries, as the tendency to relapse amounts probably to not less than 90 per cent. of the so-called cures.

The Table which follows shews the duration of disease previous to admission in the cases admitted, their condition as to curability, and the number of those who have already recovered.

Table VIII.—*Duration of Disease previous to Admission, and Condition of those Admitted.*

DURATION OF DISEASE.	INCURABLE.		CURABLE.		ALREADY DISMISSED CURED.	
	Males.	Fem.	Males.	Fem.	Males.	Fem.
Under 1 week,	3	3	7	13	5	8
,, 2 ,,	2	2	10	14	6	5
,, 3 ,,	1	3	0	5	1	3
,, 1 month,	3	5	4	5	2	1
,, 2 ,,	4	3	3	4	2	2
,, 3 ,,	2	3	2	1	0	0
,, 4 ,,	3	1	0	1	0	1
,, 5 ,,	0	0	0	1	0	0
,, 6 ,,	8	1	2	1	2	0
,, 9 ,,	3	1	2	1	1	0
,, 12 ,,	4	1	0	0	0	0
,, 18 ,,	5	3	1	1	0	0
,, 2 years,	5	6	0	1	0	1
,, 3 ,,	5	1	1	0	0	0
,, 4 ,,	3	3	1	1	0	0
,, 5 ,,	2	2	0	0	0	0
,, 6 ,,	2	1	0	0	0	0
,, 7 ,,	1	0	0	0	0	0
,, 8 ,,	2	2	0	0	0	0
,, 10 ,,	1	0	0	0	0	0
,, 12 ,,	3	0	0	0	0	0
,, 15 ,,	0	1	0	0	0	0
,, 20 ,,	1	2	0	0	0	0
Congenital, .	5	1	0	0	0	0
Unknown, .	10	19	7	4	1	1
	78	64	40	53	20	22
Total, .	142		93		42	

From this return it appears that 142 of the cases admitted laboured under an incurable form of insanity, and 93 were considered curable. Of these 93, 42 have been already discharged recovered, being 45 per cent. of the cases; or if we take those cases only which had not been affected more than six months previous to admission, those who have already left well during the year amount to upwards of 50 per cent., shewing the very great advantages of early removal to an Asylum in most cases of insanity.

Table IX. shews the period of residence in the Institution of the 91 patients who were restored.

Of the whole cases, one gentleman had been eight years an inmate of the house, one lady nearly six, and another nearly three years. Eight patients had been under two years in the house, and all the rest recovered within a year of their admission.

TABLE IX.—*Period of Residence of those Discharged Recovered.*

PERIOD OF RESIDENCE.	Males.	Females.	TOTAL.
Under 1 month . .	2	1	3
„ 2 „ . .	4	4	8
„ 3 „ . .	6	9	15
„ 4 „ . .	10	4	14
„ 5 „ . .	4	2	6
„ 6 „ . .	2	6	8
„ 7 „ . .	5	2	7
„ 8 „ . .	2	4	6
„ 9 „ . .	3	2	5
„ 10 „ . .	2	2	4
„ 11 „ . .	1	1	2
„ 12 „ . .	2	0	2
„ 18 „ . .	1	3	4
„ 2 years, . .	2	2	4
„ 3 „ . .	0	1	1
„ 6 „ . .	0	1	1
„ 8 „ . .	1	0	1
Total, . .	47	44	91

The causes of death are enumerated in the Table which follows :—

TABLE X.—*Causes of Death.*

CAUSES OF DEATH.	Males.	Females.	TOTAL.
General Paralysis, . .	10	4	14
Epilepsy, ...	5	0	5
Apoplexy, ...	1	2	3
Cerebral Effusion, . .	1	0	1
Meningitis, ...	1	1	2
Disease of Brain, . .	1	2	3
Exhaustion after Mania, .	3	1	4
„ „ Epilepsy, .	0	1	1
Empyema, ...	0	1	1
Bronchitis, . . .	1	1	2
Pneumonia, . . .	1	0	1
Phthisis, ...	11	7	18
Morbus Cordis, . . .	1	1	2
Endocarditis, . . .	1	0	1
Peritonitis, ...	0	2	2
Cancer of Peritoneum, .	1	0	1
Enteritis, ...	0	1	1
Diarrhœa, ...	1	2	3
Dysentery, ...	4	0	4
Bright's Disease, . .	1	0	1
Erysipelas, . . .	1	0	1
Senile Decay, . . .	3	0	3
Total, .	48	26	74

More than one-half of those who died may be said to have died of insanity, the immediate cause of death being some disease of the brain or nervous system. One-fourth died of Phthisis, and the remaining fourth of diseases which may be called accidental, or only remotely connected with the mental condition of the patients. The pathological appearances will be detailed in an Appendix to this Report.

The ages of those who died are contained in Table III., and the duration of their residence in the Asylum is given in the following :—

TABLE XI.—*Period of Residence of those Deceased.*

PERIOD OF RESIDENCE.	Males.	Females.	TOTAL.
One day, . .	1	0	1
Two days, . .	0	1	1
Ten ,, . .	2	0	2
Thirteen ,, . .	1	0	1
Under 1 month, . .	3	0	3
,, 2 ,, . .	4	1	5
,, 3 ,, . .	3	1	4
,, 4 ,, . .	2	1	3
,, 5 ,, . .	1	2	3
,, 6 ,, . .	1	0	1
,, 7 ,, . .	1	2	3
,, 8 ,, . .	3	1	4
,, 10 ,, . .	3	1	4
,, 11 ,, . .	0	1	1
,, 12 ,, . .	3	0	3
,, 18 ,, . .	6	3	9
,, 2 years, . .	1	2	3
,, 3 ,, . .	6	1	7
,, 4 ,, . .	3	3	6
,, 5 ,, . .	0	1	1
,, 6 ,, . .	1	1	2
,, 7 ,, . .	2	1	3
,, 9 ,, . .	1	0	1
,, 10 ,, . .	0	1	1
,, 14 ,, . .	0	1	1
,, 15 ,, . .	0	1	1
Total, . .	48	26	74

During the past year, owing partly to the unusual drought, and partly to our supply pipe being partially filled up with the sediment arising from the nature of the spring water with which the Asylum is supplied, our daily supply of water was so much diminished, that it was found necessary to procure a small engine to pump water from our own well to the cisterns. By means of this supplementary aid, we have latterly been able to obtain a sufficient supply of water for all purposes.

The new Washing-house and Laundry are finished, and have been in use for some months. The arrangements and accommodation have been found in every respect most commodious and satisfactory, although the aid of steam-power to drive our washing machine, wringing machines, and mangle, is still wanting, to make it perfectly complete. When this has been added, it is believed that the operations will be more efficiently and readily carried on, and that there will be a great saving of manual labour both for patients and servants.

Extensive operations have been carried on in the completion of the pleasure-grounds, the extension and finishing of our ornamental pond, and the laying out of the airing grounds connected with the last additions made to the Asylum. These have been made partly by means of hired labour, but mostly by the patients, to whom they have afforded a large amount of healthy occupation.

The farm and kitchen garden have, as usual, been cropped and cultivated by the patients; the pleasure grounds, flower gardens, and greenhouse, have also afforded them ample resources of this kind, while a considerable amount of trenching, and of transplanting of forest trees for the completion of our plans for the laying out of the grounds, have given full and constant occupation of the most healthy and agreeable kind to upwards of one hundred of the male patients. The little cottage at Myreside continues to afford a most agreeable retreat to a few of our inoffensive and retiring gentlemen, where they can pursue undisturbed, and without violence to their amour propre, the pleasure of gardening in their secluded garden and little greenhouse.

The statement appended to this Report of the amount of work executed by our tailors, shoemakers, printers, blacksmiths, upholsterers, glaziers, plasterers and slaters, masons, carpenters, plumbers, gasfitters, tinsmiths, and painters, with the lists of articles made and repaired by the females, will give, I think, a satisfactory proof of the industry and activity of the community, the whole of these operations, extending not only to the keeping of the house and clothing in a state of repair, but to the manufactory of innumerable articles of furniture and clothing, having been carried on by the patients, assisted by the attendants in charge of these respective departments of work.

It is scarcely necessary again to record in this Report the various sources of recreation and amusement afforded to the patients as means of solace and restoration, they have been so often enumerated in former Reports. It may suffice to say, that all the means referred to continue in active operation, and that no healthy out-door game or in-door harmless amusement that can be thought of has been left untried. The intellectual culture and exercise of the mental faculties of the inmates has been stimulated, as hitherto, by the task of sustaining our monthly periodical, and by schools and lectures, and by occasional dramatic representations. Among the lectures given was one on the Greek Mythology, for which we were indebted to Professor Blackie, and which was listened to with extreme interest. One of the inmates is now busily engaged preparing a series of beautiful diagrams to illustrate a course of lectures on the Infusoriæ. Daily walks to the country, and drives, occasional pic-nic parties, and frequent piscatorial excursions, during the season, were carried out with unprecedented animation and frequency.

Our library continues to increase partly by purchases, and partly by the kind gifts of friends, several of whom have been most liberal in their donations of books. The supply of newspapers, periodicals, and tracts, has been kept up on the same liberal scale as formerly. The galleries and sitting rooms have been decorated by a considerable number of coloured prints, which add much to the cheerfulness of the interior, and of which it is to be desired that we had a much more liberal sprinkling over our walls.

The whole Institution has been twice carefully inspected by her Majesty's Commissioners in Lunacy, who expressed, in the minutes of their visit, their satisfaction with the condition of the patients, and of the Asylum, and of its general management.

In fine, it is with pleasure that I look back upon the history of the Institution during the past year, confident that it has conferred much happiness upon many sufferers, has been the means of restoring many to themselves and to society, and that I am enabled to assure you, that the various officers and servants have shewn a praiseworthy anxiety and attention in the discharge of their respective duties.

I beg to thank the Managers for their kind co-operation with me in carrying out the great ends of the Institution, and to express a confident hope that under their management it may continue to increase in reputation and usefulness.

DAVID SKAE, M.D.

CHAPLAIN'S REPORT.

In presenting a report for the past year, it is the duty of the Chaplain to speak favourably with respect to religious matters in the Asylum; and it must be agreeable and pleasing to the Managers and other well-wishers of the Institution to learn that the inmates evidence much general decorum of conduct, and a very creditable regard to their religious duties. The attendance at the services on the Sabbath is large and proper, as well as at prayer in the Chapel on the mornings of week days; and almost in every instance, those who are present shew the highest propriety and decorum of behaviour, whilst the Psalmody is conducted in a manner truly pleasing and devotional. It has often been remarked by strangers who were present at these services, that more quietness prevails than is generally witnessed among as many people who are assembled for like purposes in any place of worship, and that their behaviour is more solemn and regular than is beheld in other places where people are assembled for similar purposes. Without pronouncing an opinion in this matter, the Chaplain may at least say, that the congregation in Morningside Asylum conduct themselves in a manner deserving of all commendation and respect. Visitors who have seen them in their several apartments, and heard and witnessed their conduct in the refractory wards, have been quite astonished to see the same individuals taking their places in the

Chapel, and shewing the greatest quietness and propriety. The clerical friends who have officiated for the Chaplain from time to time, have uniformly spoken of the great pleasure and satisfaction they experienced in addressing such a congregation; and the hearers, on the other hand, have felt pleased, and edified, and instructed, by the judicious discourses and proper exhortations of those gentlemen. Their remarks are marked by kindness, and are neither hypercritical nor severe. There is every reason to believe that they are comforted and improved by listening to the exposition of the truth, when it is done with quietness and faithfulness; and that they are instructed and enabled to proceed in the way of truth and righteousness. Whilst the terrors of the law are not to be lost sight of, the spirit of the gospel will generally speak with a prevailing voice; and whilst we may not be able fully to understand the operations of the Spirit, we believe that persons may be under the influence of the truth and taught of God, though these influences are oftentimes as gentle as the dew. There is such a thing as a "still small voice," as well as the "strong wind which rends the mountains," and the former may be as wonderful in its effects as the earthquake and the fire. When people are regular in their attendance upon the means of grace, they have reason to expect the Divine blessing; for the Lord God is a sun and a shield; the Lord will give grace and glory, and will withhold no good thing from them that walk uprightly.

The Chaplain has equal reason to speak favourably of his visits to the desponding, the sick, and the dying; and he finds, from time to time, the stern and the unbending subdued under the influence of affliction, so that they who formerly were averse to any subject of a solemn and a sacred nature, have evinced a desire after religious instruction, and have received with thankfulness his visits and his prayers. He has seldom found that perseverance in shewing a sincere desire for the spiritual welfare of the distressed, has not had a truly beneficial effect, and that when persons are convinced that their own advantage is only sought to be promoted, their dispositions are generally improved, and their bad feelings removed.

The inmates have been furnished with books and tracts of a proper kind by the Religious Tract Society, and other parties, which they have found not only interesting, but instructive. The *Leisure Hour* and the *Sunday at Home* still continue to maintain their interest, and it is scarcely possible to conceive any works more suitable to the condition of all. They communicate a vast amount of instruction in language the most plain and easily understood; their illustrations are beautiful; and their whole contents are calculated to improve the mind, while there is nothing to offend the feelings of the most sensitive. A great number of the inmates of the Institution possess much intelligence and general information, and it is of much consequence that their minds should be properly studied and directed.

The want of a separate place for worship is still felt more and more; and from the complaints that are made on this subject, the Chaplain is persuaded that a Chapel would increase the number of the congregation, add to their devotional feelings, and strengthen his own hands. This subject is so frequently brought under his notice, that he cannot allow this opportunity to pass without a word of comment.

The Officers of the Institution seem all very anxious to do what is right, and to promote the comfort and welfare of all the inmates; and the attendants and servants behave in such a manner, as to call forth the approbation of those who witness their correct conduct.

In conclusion, the Chaplain desires to express his warmest thanks to the Managers of the Institution, and other officials, for the kindness and support he always received at their hands, and their sincere and earnest attempts to promote the peace and welfare of all connected with the Asylum.

ROB. LORIMER.

ABSTRACT OF PROVISIONS, &c., ISSUED IN ROYAL EDINBURGH ASYLUM FOR THE YEAR 1858.

ARTICLES.	WESTERN DEPARTMENT. For Quarters ending— Mar. 31.	June 30.	Sept. 30.	Dec. 31.	Total in W. D.	EASTERN DEPARTMENT. For Quarters ending— Mar. 31.	June 30.	Sept. 30.	Dec. 31.	Total in E. D.	TOTAL FOR BOTH DEPARTMENTS.	
	lbs. oz.	lbs. oz.	lbs. oz.	lbs. oz.	lbs. oz.	lbs. oz.	lbs. oz.	lbs. oz.	lbs. oz.	lbs. oz.		lbs. oz.
Roasting Meat	702 ..	711 8	731 ..	732 8	2877 ..	2419 4	2425 ..	2405 8	2432 4	9682 ..	Roasting Meat,	12559 ..
Boiling Meat	6092 ..	6102 ..	6489 ..	6405 ..	25088 ..	2184 ..	2156 ..	2123 ..	2071 ..	8534 ..	Boiling Meat,	33622 ..
Salt Beef,	49 8	19 4	.. ..	8 ..	76 12	25 8	16 ..	15 8	13 ..	70 ..	Salt Beef,	146 12
Houghs	9507 ..	9862 12	10116 ..	9867 ..	39352 12	301 4	322 ..	391 12	411 8	1426 8	Houghs	40779 4
Ox Heads	12996 ..	13348 ..	13680 ..	13338 ..	53362 ..	.. ..	.. ..	.. ..	.. ..	.. ..	Ox Heads	53362 ..
Pork Ham	39 10	57 11	121 14	47 10	266 12	95 13	150 4	315 10	99 2	660 13	Pork Ham	927 9
Suet	199 ..	177 ..	161 ..	188 ..	725 ..	4 ..	.. ..	.. ..	.. ..	4 ..	Suet	729 ..
Oatmeal	14342 ..	14469 ..	14469 ..	14845 ..	58125 ..	644 ..	469 ..	560 ..	735 ..	2408 ..	Oatmeal	60533 ..
Flour	2464 ..	2520 ..	2676 ..	2364 ..	10024 ..	266 ..	236 ..	224 ..	284 ..	1010 ..	Flour	11034 ..
Barley	5331 8	5760 ..	5442 ..	5466 ..	21999 8	247 8	260 ..	201 ..	348 ..	1056 8	Barley	23056 ..
Split Pease	1886 ..	1656 ..	2087 ..	2324 ..	7953 ..	237 ..	204 ..	198 ..	234 ..	873 ..	Split Pease	8826 ..
Whole Rice	974 ..	929 ..	864 ..	910 ..	3677 ..	156 ..	154 ..	255 ..	193 ..	758 ..	Whole Rice	4435 ..
Ground Rice	.. ..	.. ..	.. ..	.. ..	.. ..	84 ..	70 ..	28 ..	42 ..	224 ..	Ground Rice	224 ..
Sago	.. ..	.. ..	.. ..	.. ..	.. ..	84 ..	14 ..	42 ..	56 ..	196 ..	Sago	196 ..
Arrow Root	511 ..	420 8	568 ..	470 ..	1969 8	78 ..	76 ..	40 ..	28 ..	222 ..	Arrow Root	2191 8
Tapioca	.. ..	.. ..	.. ..	.. ..	.. ..	84 ..	76 ..	14 ..	56 ..	230 ..	Tapioca	230 ..
Tea	197 4	213 12	223 4	229 2	863 6	184 2	192 1	200 3	191 8	767 14	Tea	1631 4
Coffee	1189 12	1231 8	1198 14	1164 8	4784 10	117 10	121 10	122 8	123 ..	484 12	Coffee	5269 6
Raw Sugar	3399 8	3514 4	3528 8	3550 4	13992 8	1128 ..	1157 8	1209 ..	1224 4	4718 12	Raw Sugar	18711 4
Loaf Sugar	110 ..	105 ..	112 ..	138 ..	465 ..	237 ..	248 ..	407 12	275 ..	1167 12	Loaf Sugar	1632 12
Fresh Butter	58 8	58 8	58 8	61 ..	236 8	191 8	195 ..	203 ..	216 8	806 ..	Fresh Butter	1042 8
Salt Butter	970 8	1010 8	1008 ..	1065 ..	4054 ..	669 ..	672 ..	660 8	679 ..	2680 8	Salt Butter	6734 8
Cheese	303 12	313 8	293 12	378 ..	1289 ..	224 3	272 8	210 ..	261 ..	967 11	Cheese	2256 11
Common Salt	3136 ..	2688 ..	3136 ..	3372 ..	12332 ..	448 ..	336 ..	448 ..	472 ..	1704 ..	Common Salt	14036 ..
Mustard	54 ..	72 ..	21 ..	66 ..	213 ..	18 ..	18 ..	24 ..	12 ..	72 ..	Mustard	285 ..
Pepper	56 ..	42 ..	28 ..	60 ..	186 ..	14 ..	.. ..	28 ..	16 ..	58 ..	Pepper	244 ..
Currants	140 ..	84 ..	84 ..	140 ..	448 ..	.. ..	.. ..	28 ..	56 ..	84 ..	Currants	532 ..
Candles	105 ..	49 ..	45 ..	83 ..	282 ..	73 ..	41 ..	25 ..	60 ..	199 ..	Candles	481 ..
Starch	175 12	157 8	239 8	195 ..	767 12	8 ..	.. ..	17 8	10 8	36 ..	Starch	803 12
Soda	1450 ..	1866 ..	2474 ..	2444 ..	8234 ..	189 ..	118 ..	111 ..	166 ..	584 ..	Soda	8820 ..
White Soap	175 8	175 8	175 8	175 8	702 ..	.. ..	.. ..	.. ..	.. ..	.. ..	White Soap	702 ..
Yellow Soap	2455 12	3244 8	3121 ..	3480 8	12301 12	193 ..	204 8	202 8	180 ..	780 ..	Yellow Soap	13081 12
Soft Soap	832 ..	832 ..	832 ..	832 ..	3328 ..	128 ..	128 ..	128 ..	128 ..	512 ..	Soft Soap	3840 ..
Molasses,	42 ..	.. ..	14 ..	14 ..	70 ..	14 ..	14 ..	14 ..	14 ..	56 ..	Molasses,	126 ..
Currant Loaves	.. ..	.. ..	.. ..	100 ..	100 ..	.. ..	.. ..	.. ..	28 ..	28 ..	Currant Loaves	128 ..
Cakes Short Bread	.. ..	.. ..	.. ..	50 ..	50 ..	.. ..	.. ..	.. ..	20 ..	20 ..	Cakes Short Bread	70 ..
4 lb. Loaves Bread	4295 ..	4680 ..	4563 ..	4635 ..	18173 ..	2225 ..	2095 ..	2225 ..	2290 ..	8835 ..	4 lb. Loaves Bread	27008 ..
6 oz. Loaves Bread	115800 ..	127700 ..	122500 ..	106100 ..	472100 ..	.. ..	.. ..	.. ..	.. ..	.. ..	6 oz. Loaves Bread	472100 ..
Sweet Milk, gals.	1530 ..	1547 ..	1599½ ..	1610 ..	6286½ ..	832½ ..	841¼	848 ..	851 ..	3373¼ ..	Sweet Milk, gals.	10659¾ ..
Skimmed Milk, do.	3240 ..	3276 ..	3312 ..	3312 ..	13140 ..	13 ..	13 ..	13 ..	13⅓ ..	52⅓ ..	Skimmed Milk, do.	13192⅓ ..
Eggs, doz.	141 ..	169 ..	187 ..	238 ..	735 ..	151 ..	145½ ..	153½ ..	177½ ..	627½ ..	Eggs, doz.	1362½ ..
Table Salt, packets	12 ..	18 ..	12 ..	12 ..	54 ..	12 ..	36 ..	12 ..	12 ..	72 ..	Table Salt, packets	126 ..
Vinegar, bottles	116 ..	100 ..	108 ..	45 ..	369 ..	30 ..	36 ..	54 ..	26 ..	146 ..	Vinegar, bottles	515 ..
Ketchup, do.	10 ..	19 ..	9 ..	8 ..	46 ..	17 ..	32 ..	16 ..	8 ..	73 ..	Ketchup, do.	119 ..
Biscuits, doz.			10	14	24	22	45	27	34	128	Biscuits, doz.	152 ..

ANDREW LESLIE, *House Superintendent*

ARTICLES	EASTERN DEPARTMENT					WESTERN DEPARTMENT					TOTAL FOR BOTH DEPARTMENTS	
	Mar. 31.	June 30.	Sept. 30.	Dec. 31	TOTAL IN E. D.	Mar. 31.	June 30.	Sept. 30.	Dec. 31.	TOTAL IN W. D.		
Apples,			5	14	19			15		15	34 pecks	Apples.
Artichokes,	24		17	70	111	12			17	29	140 gallons	Artichokes, Jer.
Beans,			73		73			273	20	293	366 pecks	Beans.
Beetroot,	19	18	24	53	114	34	17	45	54	150	264 dozen	Beetroot.
Brocoli,	22	154	21	98	295	10	69		49	128	423 dozen	Brocoli.
Brussels Sprouts,	12			32	44				16	16	60 gallons	Brussels Sprouts.
Cabbage,	273	295	284	221	1073	580	328	648	432	1988	3061 dozen	Cabbage.
Carrots,	289	183	285	272	1029	220	114	610	312	1256	2285 dozen	Carrots.
Cauliflower,			112	87	199	7		68	12	87	286 dozen	Cauliflower.
Celery,	87	92		45	224	36	37		27	100	324 bundles	Celery.
Cress,		17	25		42		17	14		31	73 bundles	Cress.
Currants,			175		175			19		19	194 pints	Currants.
Gooseberries,		80	210		290			142		142	432 pints	Gooseberries.
German Greens,	172	87		73	332	205	225	73	22	525	857 dozen	German Greens.
Kidney Beans,			32		32			6		6	38 gallons	Kidney Beans.
Leeks,	414	375		93	882	623	577		337	1537	2419 bundles	Leeks.
Lettuce,		63	57		120		34	57	46	137	257 dozen	Lettuce.
Onions,	72	18	23	57	170	67	93		45	205	375 pecks	Onions.
Ditto, Bundles,		242	412	79	733		207	758	97	1062	1795 bundles	Ditto.
Parsley,	162	231	273	185	851	42	97	51	37	227	1078 bundles	Parsley.
Parsnip,	92	57		41	190	124	112		108	344	534 dozen	Parsnip.
Pears,			48		48			24		24	72 pecks	Pears.
Pease,		22	294		316			460	45	505	811 pecks	Pease.
Potatoes,	1247	995	1076	1407	4725	3939	2105	3664	6583	16291	21016 pecks	Potatoes.
Radishes,		52	98		150		113	23	136	136	286 bundles	Radishes.
Rhubarb,		154	76		230		97	103	10	210	440 bundles	Rhubarb.
Red Cabbage,			27	56	83				28	28	112 dozen	Red Cabbage.
Savoy,	236	172		84	492	297	139		28	464	956 dozen	Savoy.
Spinach,		27	68	24	119		13			13	132 gallons	Spinach.
Strawberries,		98	113		211		40	166		206	417 pints	Strawberries.
Turnip,	187	172	445	296	1100	587	393	341	290	1611	2711 dozen	Turnip.

JAMES ROBERTSON, *Gardener.*

STATEMENT OF WORK

DONE AT

THE ROYAL EDINBURGH ASYLUM,

During the Year ending 31st December, 1858.

The whole of the work is estimated by charging journeymen's wages only.

I. TAILORS.

Making and mounting 232 new suits, at 6s. 6d. each,	L.75 8 0	
Repairs, ...	69 9 3	
New work and repairs for private individuals, .	12 15 1	
		L.157 12 4

II. SHOEMAKERS.

Making 239 pairs of men's shoes, at 4s.,	.	L.47 16 0		
„ 162 „	women's do., at 2s. 6d.,	.	20 5 0	
„ 21 „	do. lacing do., at 3s.,	.	3 3 0	
„ 47 „	carpet shoes, at 1s.,	.	2 7 0	
„ 3 „	men's boots, at 5s., .	.	0 15 0	
„ 1 „	do. do. at 5s. 6d.,	.	0 5 6	
„ 3 „	women's lock boots, at 3s. 3d.,		0 9 9	
„ 4 „	do. do. at 3s. 6d.,		0 14 0	
„ 135 „	braces, at 3d.,	.	1 13 9	
Repairs for males, L.30, 16s. 11d.—females, L.8, 19s. 11d., ...			39 16 10	
New work and repairs for private individuals, .			15 15 10	
				133 1 8

III. MASONS.

Building, cutting, slapping, altering, and repairing sundry places; altering, lifting, and relaying pavement in Western Department, ...	L.16 10 9	
Do. do. do. in Eastern Department,	12 18 5	
Do. do. do. in miscellaneous buildings,	6 17 9	
		36 6 11

Carry forward,	.	L.327 0 11

41

Brought forward, . L.327 0 11

IV. GLAZIERS, PLASTERERS, & SLATERS.

Putting in 2044 panes of glass in Western Depart-
ment, ... L.17 4 3
Do. 95 do. in Eastern Department, 2 2 11
Do. 46 do. in miscellaneous buildings, 0 18 4
Do. 8 do. in garden and workshops, 0 19 7
Plaster, slating, and painting work, . . 20 0 5
             41 5 6

V. PRINTERS.

Annual Report for the year 1858, . . L.20 4 2
Monthly Mirror, with title and contents, . 15 10 2
Receipts, directions, diet tables, reports, circulars
for Treasurer, order books, labels, laundry and
clothes' lists, office-bearers and visitors' cards,
daily returns, Physician's returns, ball orders,
programmes, warrants, contracts, passes, and
other sundries for Western Department, . 30 1 8
All Sorts, poetry, &c. for Eastern Department, 11 1 6
             76 17 6

VI. CARPENTERS.

Making wardrobe, press for laundry, dressing tables, forms
for galleries, cover for well, fittings for stable, stands for
sinks, new doors and standards, covers for baths, frames for
bed stretchers, window shutters, bason stands, frames, ven-
tilators, water spouts for the pond, palings, linings, flooring,
new window frames, bottle rack, cornices, window blind rol-
lers; cleaning, altering, and repairing wardrobe, bookcase,
meat hoist, and various other sundries in Western Department, ... L.89 6 2
Making a new hen house, 6 mahogany fire screens,
tub, covers for baths, wash-hand stands, ventila-
tors, bed stretchers, gate for garden, 10 new
mantelpieces, stands for sinks, &c.; also altering
and repairing shelves, tables, chairs, window
blinds, and various other sundries in Eastern
Department, ... 26 5 5
Making and repairing wheelbarrows, pick, rake,
spade, and plough handles, garden palings, &c.
for garden; flaps, &c. for piggery; moulds,
hammer handles, hurley, patterns for smiths,
steps, and sundry other articles, . . 7 10 1
Making and altering various jobs at miscellaneous
buildings, ... 4 3 8
Amount for coffins, ... 6 10 0
             133 15 4

Carry forward, . L.578 19 3

F

Brought forward, . . L.578 19 3

VII. ENGINEERS AND BLACKSMITHS.

Amount of engineer and blacksmith's work for Western Department, ...	L.83	9	9	
Do. do. for Eastern Department, .	14	7	4	
Do. do. for miscellaneous buildings,	6	0	8	
Do. do. for workshops and garden,	5	19	4	
				109 17 1

VIII. PLUMBERS, GASFITTERS, & TINSMITHS.

Plumber's work for Western Department, .	L.31	13	10	
Gasfitter's do. do. .	12	16	8	
Tinsmith's do. do. . .	6	14	0	
Plumber's work for Eastern Department, .	15	0	11	
Gasfitter's do. do. . .	2	17	6	
Tinsmith's do. do. . .	2	5	3	
Plumber and gasfitter's work for miscellaneous buildings, ...	6	7	0	
Do. do. for garden and workshops,	0	12	6	
				78 7 8

IX. PAINTERS.

Painting and papering Western Department,	L.103	2	4½	
Do. do. Eastern Department,	61	5	9½	
Do. do. miscellaneous buildings,	4	6	6	
				168 14 8

X. UPHOLSTERERS.

Making new hair and sea-weed mattresses, pillows, straw palliasses, covering chairs, canvass frames, strapping, &c.; also altering, stuffing, twilting, and repairing old do. for the Western Department, ... L.74 10 1
Making and repairing do. for Eastern Department, 16 2 0

90 12 1

L.1026 10 9

ANDREW LESLIE, *House Superintendent.*

ARTICLES MADE BY FEMALES IN WESTERN DEPARTMENT.

			L.	s.	d.					L.	s.	d.
Printed gowns,	. at	1s. 8d.	23	6	8			Brought forward,		81	16	8
Silk do.	. „	3s. 6d.	1	15	0	242	Pair of shoes					
Night gowns,	. „	0s. 6d.	4	11	0		(bound), .	. at	0s. 2d.	2	0	4
Caps, . .	. „	0s. 3d.	3	8	6	17	Veils knitted,	. „	1s. 0d.	0	17	0
Dress caps,	. „	1s. 0d.	0	9	0	22	Bonnets trimmed,	„	0s. 3d.	0	5	6
Polkas, .	. „	2s. 0d.	0	10	0	730	Sheets hemmed,	. „	0s. 2d.	6	1	8
Twilted petticoats,	„	0s. 8d.	0	19	4	345	Pillow cases,	. „	0s. 2d.	2	17	6
Drugget do.	„	0s. 3d.	1	14	9	49	Roller towels,	. „	0s. 1d.	0	4	1
Flannel do.	„	0s. 3d.	2	3	6	243	Common do.,	. „	0s. 1d.	1	0	3
Flannel shifts,	. „	0s. 9d.	9	10	6	405	Pair of blankets,	„	0s. 4d.	6	15	0
Shifts, .	. „	0s. 3d.	0	12	6	265	Plaiding jackets,	„	0s. 9d.	9	18	9
Pair of drawers,	„	0s. 9d.	7	2	6	17	Chair covers,	. „	1s. 0d.	0	17	0
Slip bodices,	. „	0s. 6d.	0	4	0	77	Bed covers,	. „	0s. 4d.	1	5	8
Habit shirts,	. „	0s. 3d.	0	3	0	50	Table cloths,	. „	0s. 2d.	0	8	4
Knitted tidies,	. „	1s. 0d.	0	9	0	540	Dozen of buttons,	„	0s. 1d.	2	5	0
Sewed collars,	. „	0s. 6d.	1	10	0	36	Yards of muslin					
Silk cloaks,	. „	3s. 6d.	0	7	0		figured, .	. „	1s. 0d.	1	16	0
Neckerchiefs,	. „	0s. 2d.	0	11	4	7	Set of window					
Pocket handker-							drapery, .	. „	3s. 0d.	1	1	0
chiefs, .	. „	0s. 1d.	0	1	6	4	Window blinds, .	„	0s. 6d.	0	2	0
Aprons (females),	„	0s. 2d.	3	6	10	11	Set of bed curtains,	„	6s. 0d.	3	6	0
Do. (males),	„	0s. 3d.	0	15	9	8	Pair of slippers, .	„	1s. 6d.	0	12	0
Striped shirts,	. „	0s. 4d.	9	16	8	12	Pin cushions,	. „	0s. 6d.	0	6	0
White dresses,	. „	1s. 6d.	3	0	0	2	Wine rubbers,	. „	0s. 4d.	0	0	8
Pair of stockings,	„	0s. 4d.	5	8	4	2	Trousers, .	. „	1s. 6d.	0	3	0
	Carry forward,	L.81	16	8					L.123	19	5	

ARTICLES REPAIRED BY FEMALES IN WESTERN DEPARTMENT.

			L.	s.	d.					L.	s.	d.
5 Shirts,	. at	0s. 2d.	12	11	8			Brought forward,		35	6	3
8 Gowns,	. . „	0s. 2d.	4	1	4	11820	Pair of stockings, at	0s. 1d.		49	5	0
0 Night gowns,	. „	0s. 2d.	4	6	8	901	Sheets, .	. „	0s. 1d.	3	15	1
9 Shifts,	. . „	0s. 2d.	5	4	10	140	Pillow cases,	. „	0s. 1d.	0	11	8
6 Aprons,	. . „	0s. 1d.	2	1	4	379	Pair of blankets,	„	0s. 2d.	3	3	2
7 Pair of stays,	. „	0s. 2d.	0	2	10	37	Bed covers,	. „	0s. 2d.	0	6	2
4 Pair of drawers,	„	0s. 2d.	0	0	8	8	Carpets and					
8 Petticoats,	. „	0s. 2d.	6	3	0		mats, .	. „	3s. 2d.	1	5	4
7 Caps,	. . „	0s. 1d.	0	13	11	3	Table cloths,	. „	0s. 10d.	0	2	6
	Carry forward,	L.35	6	3					L.93	15	2	

ARTICLES MADE BY FEMALES IN EASTERN DEPARTMENT.

2 Set of bed curtains.	30 Binding blankets.	17 Petticoats.
46 Quilts.	64 Towels.	11 Dresses.
6 Bolster cases.	63 Aprons.	68 Caps.
100 Pillow cases.	41 Chemises.	30 Habit shirts.
110 Sheets.	12 Bed gowns.	14 Collars.
20 Blankets.	16 Underdresses.	3 Pair slippers embroidere

ARTICLES REPAIRED BY FEMALES IN EASTERN DEPARTMENT.

469 Pair stockings.	51 Dresses.	64 Pillow cases.
19 Pair stays.	60 Underdresses.	76 Quilts.
66 Petticoats.	59 Habit Shirts.	76 Sheets.
47 Aprons.	48 Night caps.	417 Shirts.
46 Bed gowns.	71 Blankets.	9 Bonnets.
67 Chemises.		

J. U. MACDOUGALL, *Matron.*

ABSTRACT, &c., VALUE OF STOCK ON HAND IN STORES
AT 31st DECEMBER, 1858.

1. Provisions, stimulants, groceries, &c., ... L.177 6
2. House Furnishings—Consisting of upholsterer's and plumber's stock, blankets, counterpanes, Hessian, bed lace, table napkins, sheets, towels, pillow cases, table cloths, sheeting, damask cloth, toilet covers, tubs, pails, clothes' baskets, sponges, spoons, knives, dressing glasses, glass globes for gas, brushes, tin goods, matts, hair pillows, combs, china, crockery, and crystal, ... 282 4
3. Male Clothing—Consisting of tailor's and shoemaker's stock, plaiding, white and black cotton, lasting, twill, blue and black cloth, canvass, packsheet and sail cloth, corduroy, striped shirting, white, black, and brown linen, jean, drill, hose, tweeds, flannel drawers and jackets, night caps, black sewing silk, handkerchiefs, carpet bags, vests, stocks, bonnets, braces, and shoes, ... 196 16
4. Female Clothing—Consisting of apron checks, railway stripe, muslin, drugget, flannel shawls, tapes, cotton reels, worsted, stays, thimbles, buttons, aprons, needles, hooks and eyes, pins, prints, laces, . 95 1
5. Ironmongery, &c.—Consisting of nails and tacks, hinges, tools, coffin mountings, screw nails, glue, sandpaper, twine, locks, &c.; also printer's, glazier's, mason's, painter's, carpenter's, and smith's stock, 120 17
6. Amount of pigs, per valuation, ... 127 15

L.1000 1

ANDREW LESLIE, *House Superintendent.*

APPENDIX.

PATHOLOGICAL APPEARANCES OBSERVED IN THE BRAIN DURING THE YEAR 1858.

Of the 84 deaths which occurred during the year, the pathological appearances have been noted in 30 cases, and the lesions of the Encephalon carefully recorded. To shew the relation of these lesions to the different forms of mental disorder, they have been, as usual, arranged in a statistical form.

The subjoined Tables shew the forms of insanity, and the causes of death, in those examined.

FORMS OF INSANITY.

Congenital Imbecility,	. . 2	Brought forward,	.	10
Acute Mania,	. . . 1	Melancholia, . . .	.	4
Chronic Mania,	. , . 1	Monomania of Suspicion, .	.	6
Dementia,	. . . 5	Do. Unseen Agency,		2
Epileptic Dementia, .	. . 1	General Paralysis, .	.	8
Carry forward,	. 10	Total,	.	30

CAUSES OF DEATH.

Apoplexy,	. . . 1	Brought forward,	.	21
Cerebral Softening, .	. . 1	Valvular Disease of Heart,	.	1
General Paralysis,	. . 8	Dysentery, . . .	.	2
Cerebral Effusion,	. . 1	Cancer of Peritoneum,	.	2
Tubercular Meningitis,	. . 1	Bright's Disease, .	.	2
Phthisis,	 7	Phlegmonous Erysipelas,	.	1
Chronic Pleurisy,	. . 1	Pyæmia, . . .	.	1
Endocarditis, .	. . 1			
Carry forward,	. 21	Total,	.	30

The Calvarium was of unusual thickness in 1 case of General Paralysis.

The Calvarium was thinner than usual in 1 case of General Paralysis.

The Dura Mater was very adherent to the Calvarium in 1 case of Acute Mania, 1 of Dementia, and 1 of Melancholia.

Spicula of Bone were found in the Falx Cerebri in 2 cases of Monomania of Suspicion, and 1 of General Paralysis.

The Membranes were congested in 1 case of Acute Mania, 1 of Melancholia, and 1 of General Paralysis.

A thin layer of Blood lined the inner surface of the Dura Mater over the Right Hemisphere in 1 case of General Paralysis.

Opacity and Thickening of the Arachnoid were observed in 1 case of Congenital Imbecility, 1 of Chronic Mania, 5 of Dementia, 1 of Melancholia, 1 of Monomania of Suspicion, 1 of Monomania of Unseen Agency, and 6 of General Paralysis.

Tubercle was deposited in the Arachnoid in 1 case of Monomania of Suspicion, and 1 of General Paralysis.

The Contiguous Surfaces of the Arachnoid were adherent in 1 case of General Paralysis.

Subarachnoid Effusion was present in 1 case of Chronic Mania, 3 of Dementia, 2 of Monomania of Suspicion, and 6 of General Paralysis, in one of which the effusion was sero-sanguineous.

Fibrin was deposited on the Base of the Brain, chiefly over the Pons Varolii and Cerebellum, in 1 case of Monomania of Suspicion; over the Cerebellum only, in 1 case of General Paralysis.

The Convolutions were remarkably flattened in 1 case of Dementia.

The Lateral Ventricles contained a considerable amount of Fluid in 3 cases of Dementia, 2 of Monomania of Suspicion, and 3 of General Paralysis.

The Lining Membrane of the Lateral Ventricles presented a granular appearance in 1 case of Dementia, and 3 of General Paralysis. A similar appearance was observed in the Fourth Ventricle in 1 case of Dementia, 1 of Melancholia, 2 of Monomania of Suspicion, and 2 of General Paralysis.

The Surfaces of the Optic Thalami were remarkably puckered in 1 case of Chronic Mania, 2 of Monomania of Suspicion, and 1 of General Paralysis.

The Cerebral Substance was Anæmic in 1 case of Dementia, 2 of Monomania of Suspicion, and 1 of General Paralysis.

The White Substance was tougher than usual in 1 case of Dementia, 1 of Monomania of Suspicion, and 6 of General Paralysis.

The Grey Substance was adherent to the Membranes in 4 cases of General Paralysis; it was violaceous in tint in 1 case of Monomania of Suspicion.

The Cerebral Substance was generally softened in 1 case of Dementia, 2 of Monomania of Suspicion, and 1 of General Paralysis.

The Pillars of the Fornix were very much softened in 1 case of General Paralysis.

The Floor of the Fourth Ventricle was softened in 1 case of Melancholia.

The Cerebral Vessels were Atheromatous in 1 case of Dementia, and 1 of General Paralysis.

A node-like Process projected from the Right Temporal Bone over the Superior Semicircular Canal in 1 case of Monomania of Unseen Agency.

In the case of an emaciated man, 60 years of age, who had been for many years of most penurious habits and hoarding disposition, and who had laboured under Acute Mania for the last ten days of his life, death was the result of an apoplectic seizure, which preceded the fatal event by ten hours. The following were the morbid appearances presented by the Encephalon:—The Dura Mater was firmly adherent to the Calvarium over the whole upper surface, and the membranes much congested throughout. The substance of the middle and posterior lobes of the right hemisphere were completely broken up by a clot weighing about 6 oz., which extended to within a quarter of an inch of the lateral surface of the brain externally, and internally was separated from the lateral ventricle by a thin layer of optic thalamus. No extravasation had taken place into the ventricle. The substance of the brain generally was pale, and no trace of previous softening was detected in the brain immediately surrounding the clot. A small spot of old softening, however, was found in the Crus Cerebri of the left side. All the larger cerebral vessels were atheromatous.

Of the four cases in which puckering of the surface of the optic thalami was observed, section of the organs disclosed no morbid appearance in the case of General Paralysis, while in the other three the change seemed due to the presence of numerous small points of softening in the thalamus: in all the corrugation was equally distinct on both sides.

In one case of Senile Dementia, there were two depressions on the surface of the Cerebrum, each about the size of a walnut; one in the posterior third of the outer aspect of the left hemisphere, and the other in the anterior third on the same side. On removal of the membrane, it was found that the grey matter had been destroyed, and the white substance was uneven and fringy, as if the result of cerebral abscess. The Encephalon appeared otherwise normal.

In a female who had been demented for many years, no lesion of any kind was detected within the cranium; the kidneys, however, were so extensively diseased, as to retain scarcely any of their normal structure; the upper portion of the left was converted into a large cyst. Tubercle was deposited in the apices of both lungs, and several small vomicæ were found. It is perhaps worthy of note in connection with the mental disease, that the case was characterised during life by the entire absence of œdema or ascites till a very short period before death.

The annexed Table shews the weights of the different organs, and the immediate causes of death, in the cases examined.

Table of Weights of Organs, and Causes of Death.

	Age.	FORM OF INSANITY.	CAUSE OF DEATH.	Encephal.	Cerebell., Pons, and Medulla.	Heart.	Right Lung	Left Lung.	Liver.	Spleen.	Right Kidney.	Left Kidney.	Stature. ft.	Stature. in.
MALES.	53	Acute Mania,	Apoplexy,	54	6½	8	28	30	45	4	6½	6	5	4
	52	Chronic Mania,	Endocarditis,	48½	6½	17½	33	39	79	3½	5½	5	5	9
	68	Dementia,	Softening of Brain,	54½	5½	19½	36	35	42	9½	6	6	5	10
	59	Do.	Cerebral Effusion,	49	5½	7	31	29	48	3½	5½	6	5	4
	80	Do.	Phlegmonous Erysipelas,	41	5	7	32½	23	51½	7	5	5½	5	10
	16	Epileptic Dementia,	Phthisis,	46½	6	7	26	27½	54	6½	6	4½	5	9
	62	Melancholia,	Cancer of Peritoneum,	52	7	12	42½	46	59	7½	6	6	5	9
	51	Do.	Dysentery,	52	7	7½	29	26	45	5	6	5½	5	6
	53	Monomania of Suspicion,	Bright's Disease,	53	6	8	59	52	49	6½	7	6½	5	10
	58	Do. Do.	Chronic Pleurisy,	49	5½	7	56	12	48	4	5	5	5	8
	55	Do. Do.	Phthisis,	48½	6½	11½	67	36	66½	4½	5	5½	5	7
	35	Do. Do.	Dysentery,	58	6½	10	14	17	62	4	4½	5½	5	3
	30	Do. Do.	Phthisis,	50	6	8	30½	40	46	6	5½	5	5	5
	19	Congenital Imbecility,	Do.	43½	8	5½	10	8½	41	3	5	4½	5	7
	46	General Paralysis,	General Paralysis,	45	6	8½	26	21	47	3	6½	5½	5	7½
	67	Do. Do.	Do. Do.	48	6½	11½	32	21½	48	3	4	4½	5	9
	29	Do. Do.	Do. Do.	43½	6½	6	19	10	45	4½	4½	4	5	6
	54	Do. Do.	Do. Do.	49	6	15	64	47½	51	5½	5	5	5	11
	35	Do. Do.	Do. Do.	50	6½	12	43	37½	56	8	6	6½	6	1
	56	Do. Do.	Do. Do.	44½	6½	12½	32	24½	49½	5	6	7	5	8
FEMALES.	26	Dementia,	Phthisis,	54½	6½	7½	23	24½	61	2½	4½	4½	5	2
	41	Melancholia,	Pyæmia,	41½	4½	8	9½	19	40	3½	4	3½	5	3
	45	Do.	Phthisis,	47½	6	9½	33½	32	46	5	6	6	5	5
	24	Monomania of Suspicion,	Tubercular Meningitis,	52	6	9½	13	13½	31	3	4½	5	5	5
	45	Do. Unseen Agency,	Cancer of Peritoneum,	44½	5½	5½	11	11½	..	..	3	4½	5	3
	40	Do. Do.	Morbus Cordis,	39	5	9	19	13	38	5½	4½	5	5	0
	38	Congenital Imbecility,	Phthisis,	39	5	7	12½	11½	24	5	3	3½	5	0
	56	General Paralysis,	General Paralysis,	39½	5½	10	34½	32	43	3	4	5	5	6
	47	Do. Do.	Do. Do.	40½	6½	8½	25	25½	77	11½	4½	4	5	7